Are We There Yet?

by Kitty Fross

Illustrated by Gregg Schigiel

The SpongeBob Squarepants Movie was written by
Derek Drymon, Tim Hill, Steve Hillenburg,
Kent Osborne, Aaron Springer & Paul Tibbitt

SCHOLASTIC INC.

New York   Toronto   London   Auckland   Sydney
Mexico City   New Delhi   Hong Kong   Buenos Aires

Published by Scholastic Inc.,
90 Old Sherman Turnpike, Danbury, Connecticut 06816.

ISBN 0-439-69983-5

First Scholastic Printing, November 2004

Chapters

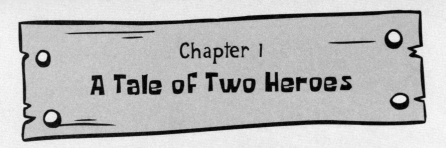

Chapter 1
A Tale of Two Heroes

"It's showtime!" SpongeBob SquarePants declared, as he strode into the Krusty Krab.

"Yay! I can't wait for my part!" Patrick Star, SpongeBob's best friend, cheered.

"Yep, it's a big night, Pat," said SpongeBob, nodding gravely. "Tonight we tell the world about our Epic Man Quest."

He walked over to the order microphone and turned up the volume full blast.

9

"Your attention, please," SpongeBob said. "We're thrilled that so many of you showed up for our little presentation."

"Presentation?" a fish asked. "I'm here for the free food. Where's my Krabby Patty sample?"

Mr. Krabs, SpongeBob's boss, leaned into the microphone. "Coming right up, just as soon as the show is over."

"Okay! If we start our program now,"
SpongeBob said, "we should be ready to take
your questions in six or seven hours, tops."

As several customers ran for the door,
Squidward Tentacles groaned. "Mr. Krabs," he
whispered. "Why are you encouraging this?"

"Well, Mr. Squidward, the boys *did* save me life," Mr. Krabs replied. "Besides, this audience is going to need plenty of food and coffee to stay awake. With me special dinner-theater rates, I'll make a fortune!"

"Let us begin our story," SpongeBob said dramatically. "Patrick, please distribute the handouts so that our audience can follow along."

SpongeBob peered intensely at the audience, then shouted, "Lights! Cue projector. Slide number one!"

Chapter 2

Evil Doings A-Brewing

The room went dark. The projector
hummed to life. SpongeBob began to tell
the story of his great adventure:

Ever since I was a little spongelet,
I've known I was destined for glory. And
then one day, it seemed as if all my dreams
were coming true. After 374 consecutive
Employee of the Month awards, I was going
to be made manager of the brand-new
Krusty Krab Two.

Or so I thought. But Mr. Krabs, in his all-knowing knowledgeness, had other plans. He wasn't looking for

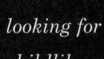

childlike enthusiasm, youthful energy, or boyish good looks. He had his sights set on

maturity. And so he gave the promotion to Squidward instead.

Of course, I took the news with my usual grace.

SpongeBob flipped on the lights.
"While we were busy at the Goofy Goober,
evil doings were a-brewing at the Chum
Bucket. Please direct your attention to
the monitor now, for what I like to call
Exhibit A. Observe."

A grainy image filled the TV screen and Plankton's voice boomed from the speakers: "Time to put Plan Z into effect!"

SpongeBob nodded knowingly, "That's right, folks. Plankton was up to his old tricks. We don't know exactly what happened next, but we have a pretty good idea. So we've created a little reenactment to bring it all to life for you. Patrick, if you will!"

Patrick stepped forward. "Hello. My name is Plankton," he read woodenly. "I have a plan to rule the world. I will steal Neptune's crown. I will sell it to Shell City and frame Eugene Krabs. Then the secret formula for the Krabby Patty will be mine. I am an evil genius. Thank you."

Chapter 3
You Don't Need a License to Drive a Sandwich

"Oh my, folks! Didn't that just give you goose bumps?" SpongeBob squeaked into the microphone.

Another group of fish hurried towards the exit. Unaware, SpongeBob flipped the lights off and continued:

King Neptune sure was mad when he discovered his crown had been stolen. Truth is, King Neptune is a little sensitive about his . . . ah . . . thinning hair.

Neptune believed Plankton's lie and
thought Mr. Krabs was the thief. So someone
had to go to Shell City and bring King
Neptune's crown back, or Mr. Krabs was
toast—burnt toast. Luckily, I knew just the
sponge for the job!

Neptune gave me just ten days to get there and back. Then my good buddy Pat offered to join me, and he even bargained for time with King Neptune. And wouldn't you know, he got old Neptune down from ten days to six!

King Neptune's daughter, Mindy, warned us about the crooks, killers, monsters, and the giant Cyclops that stood between us and victory. She told us about the poisonous gases in Shell City. And she even gave us a magical bag of winds to help us get back home with the crown.

It was going to be dangerous. It was going to be scary. It was going to separate the men from the boys. But Patrick and I were fearless. We hopped in the Patty Wagon and headed for the border.

Some people didn't believe a couple of
"kids" like us would stand a chance in the
big bad world. But boy, did we prove
them wrong!

And sure, Plankton sent a meanie hit
man guy named Dennis after us.

But luck was still on our side. We soon found the Patty Wagon parked outside of this picturesque neighborhood tavern.

Now all we had to do was retrieve our key. The problem was . . . how? The locals didn't look too friendly.

Well, you know how it is when you've got a problem to solve, and a soap dispenser catches your eye.

One bubble led to another, and before we knew it, we had a full-blown bubble party on our hands!

Turns out, the locals didn't really care for bubbles. There's just no pleasing some folks, I guess.

It all worked out just fine, though. In all the ruckus, Patrick managed to grab the key, and we were back in business!

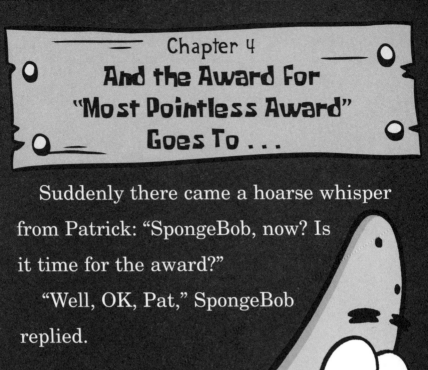

Chapter 4
And the Award For "Most Pointless Award" Goes To . . .

Suddenly there came a hoarse whisper from Patrick: "SpongeBob, now? Is it time for the award?"

"Well, OK, Pat," SpongeBob replied.

SpongeBob snapped on the lights, and Patrick stepped up to the microphone. "Uhhhh, I'm here to present a special award," he said. "The Coolest Future Monarch of the Sea and Overall Hotty Award goes to—Princess Mindy!"

There was a scattering of confused applause as an image of King Neptune's daughter appeared on the monitor.

"Thank you, Patrick," Mindy said. "I'm

sorry I can't be there in person to accept this . . . really unusual award, but thanks for saving the world and everything. You guys are great!"

"Wooooh! You rock my world, Mindy!" Patrick screamed at the top of his lungs.

But the monitor had already faded to static.

"Hey! What was the point of that?" someone in the audience grumbled.

"I have no idea," another fish replied, "But if I don't get my free Krabby Patty soon, I'm out of here!"

Mr. Krabs bustled over to the microphone. "I've got fresh coffee," he announced. "Who's ready for a refill?"

A sea of hands shot up, and Mr. Krabs eagerly began pouring. "That'll be $9 each," he said cheerily.

Chapter 5

From Boys to Men
(and Back Again)

SpongeBob stepped back up to the
microphone. "Now—back to our story. Hey,
you're all following along in your handouts,
right?" A few fish riffled sullenly through
their paper packets. SpongeBob continued:

Mindy was right. The road to Shell City is paved with dangers, like muscle-bound bar bullies, sweet little old ice cream ladies who turn into vicious predators, and some third, even more dangerous thing that I can't think of right now.

We almost gave up hope when we got to this deep, dark, dangerous, monster-infested trench. But just when we were ready to turn around and go back home like a couple of kids, Mindy showed up and used her mermaid magic to give us the courage of MEN!

With the power of our manly mustaches, we were unstoppable. Giant crabs and hideous sea monsters were no match for us!

Then on the outskirts of Shell City, things got really exciting. First Dennis, the hit man, found us and ripped off our mustaches.

And then just as he was about to stomp us, he got stomped himself . . .

. . . by the evil Cyclops! Words can't describe what happened then, which is why I've asked Patrick to handle the next part of the presentation.

Patrick stepped forward. "OK, well, this is us getting snatched up by the Cyclops," he explained.

"And this is us waking up in a scary poison-gas-filled tank of death."

48

Patrick flipped to a new page. "Now this is the part where I defeat the Cyclops, and then Mindy shows up and gives me her phone number."

"Patrick," SpongeBob hissed. "That didn't happen!"

Patrick shrugged. "You tell your part your way—I'll tell my part mine."

Chapter 6
A Hero's Not
Just a Sandwich

"Boys," Mr. Krabs broke in. "Yer losing me customers . . . I mean, yer audience. Maybe you should skip to the end!"

"But this is the best part!" SpongeBob gasped. "This is the part where we realized that we'd actually made it to Shell City after all, and then the sea creatures came back to life and battled the evil Cyclops, and then we grabbed Neptune's crown and ran for the dock, where we lost Mindy's bag of winds . . . "

"I know, SpongeBob, but . . . ," Mr. Krabs
interrupted.

" . . . and then the friendly lifeguard gave
us a ride back to Bikini Bottom, and Dennis
reappeared but we fought him off and

returned the crown to Neptune only to discover that Plankton had enslaved everyone with his evil Chum Bucket helmets and turned everyone against us . . . ," the unstoppable SpongeBob continued.

" . . . And then we saved the sea with the power of Rock 'n' Roll, and Plankton went to jail, and I got to be manager after all!" SpongeBob concluded, finally stopping to breathe.

"Yes, it's a good story, laddy," Mr. Krabs said consolingly. "But sleeping customers are bad for business. I think yer fans may be ready for a little break."

Mr. Krabs cleared his throat. "All right, folks, the show is over. It's time for yer free samples." He held up a tray of six minuscule Krabby Patties.

"That's *all* the free samples?" an angry
fish asked in disbelief.

"Now don't be shy, step right up and take
one," Mr. Krabs urged. "Like the sign says,

'while supplies last.'"

The audience leaped to its feet and
stampeded toward the door. A few lucky
fish grabbed tiny patties as they passed.

"Gee, I guess everyone had a bus to catch," Patrick said.

"But what about the Q and A and the photo op?" SpongeBob whimpered.

"Don't worry, SpongeBob," Mr. Krabs said

soothingly. "We're all grateful to ye. Ye did OK for a Knucklehead McSpazaton. Now don't forget to clean up before ye leave— SpongeBob ManagerPants!" Mr. Krabs winked, gave SpongeBob a pat on the back, and headed for the door.

SpongeBob sighed, then got to work tidying up.

"Well, Pat," he said, once the room was clean, "I guess the greatest satisfaction is a job well done." He locked the door, and the two friends headed home.

A moment passed, and then the video monitor began to hiss and flicker. An image of Plankton appeared on the screen. He shook his fist, and his voice filled the empty restaurant: "I'LL DESTROY ALL OF YOUUUUU!"